The History on the Page: Adventures in Black British History

Tony Talburt

Illustrations by Kieran Merkman

Dr Tony Talburt is a specialist in African and Caribbean studies and has research interests in international politics and development studies. He obtained his B.A Degree in History and Social Sciences from the University of the West Indies, a M.A. from the University of Warwick in International Studies and also a PhD in International Politics and Development from the London South Bank University. He has over 25 years teaching experience in schools, FE colleges and universities. His previous publications include; *Food of the Plantation Slaves of Jamaica,* 2004, Trafford Publishers and *Rum, Rivalry and Resistance: Fighting for the Caribbean Spirit,* 2010, Hansib Publishers.

Chapter One: Britain's African Emperor

It first started last summer when ten-year-old Omar and his twelve-year-old sister Zarah were sitting by the window, staring outside but looking at nothing. It was only 11 O'clock in the morning, and they were already feeling bored. Omar wondered what he would spend the day doing. He'd already spent much of the morning listening to music on his MP3 while Zarah sat at the computer linking up with some of her friends on Facebook. But forty minutes later they were bored. In fact, most weekends they were bored, as they lived in a small town and there were not many places to go or things to do in Wonderham.

After another painful thirty minutes had dragged by - when they realised that any more of this boredom would drive them insane - the children decided to ask their mum if they could go and play in the back garden in their treehouse. They decided to climb up the large oak tree to get to the treehouse that their dad had built for them last summer. This was the one place where they could always go and have fun. Their treehouse was filled with old toys and books they no longer used very often or in some cases not at all. This was their own space, where their parents had promised that very few rules would be imposed on them. Not surprisingly, this room was very untidy, as neither child could ever agree who should do the tidying up.

After a few minutes of playing darts, Omar saw a book in the corner on the floor that suddenly frightened him.

'Oh no', he cried out, 'I'm gonna get in trouble. I forgot my books for my homework at school.'

It was one of his school library books about the Roman Army in Britain. A terrified expression came over his face. He had forgotten that his history project on the Roman invasion of Britain was due on Monday and his teacher, Mrs Jules, would be very angry if the work was not done. Nobody liked to miss her homework, because she was very strict. In fact, none of the children in the class even liked her, but they dare not miss her homework. Omar loved school, but just hated history. Why would anyone want to study about people and places that didn't even exist anymore?

A very desperate Omar decided to seek help from his older sister Zarah. 'Why did the Romans have to come to Britain? And how can I find out about one great Roman Emperor?'

'Why don't you read that book in the corner?' she yelled at him, pointing to an old history book on the floor.

'That's going to be boring,' said Omar. 'Look at all these funny-looking people in this picture of strange men, dressed in costumes.' Although he hated the subject, he silently wondered to himself what it would have been like to live during those times when the Romans ruled Britain. On the page he could see soldiers on horseback riding towards the small town of York, where many Roman soldiers had once lived.

'I wish, I wish, I wish I could be part of the history on that page,' mumbled Omar. 'That would help me to understand how they lived, and perhaps I could even meet a Roman Emperor.' He kept repeating the words, 'I wish, I wish, I could be part of the history on the page.'

Then something strange started to happen. Everything in the little treehouse started to spin. The page in the book seemed to get larger and larger and the people in the picture who were on the page of the book started to move. Almost like magic, the picture in the book slowly filled the room in their treehouse - and before they knew it, both Omar and Zarah found themselves floating onto the page of the book, so they became part of the history on the page. They had been transported back in time to the period when the Romans ruled Britain. It was the year A.D. 208.

It was a cold morning in York, and the sky was dull and grey. This hardly seemed to matter to the people, because they all seemed quietly excited as they stared down the dirt-covered road. There were hundreds of people who had come to watch the Roman soldiers as they marched through the streets to finish setting up camp and a station near to York. This was where the new Emperor of England was going to live. Even though Zarah and Omar had only just arrived on the scene, they could not help but feel excited as well.

'Wow,' said Omar. 'Look at all those Roman soldiers. They are dressed exactly like the pictures we saw in the book while we were in the treehouse.'

Hundreds of soldiers dressed in brightly-coloured metallic outfits were heading towards where Zarah and Omar were standing. The dust from their dirt path road continued to rise higher as the soldiers got nearer.

Even though Zarah was not really interested in the topic about the Romans in Britain, she now seemed excited. 'Look at their weapons,' she pointed out to Omar. There were Roman foot soldiers fully armed with long javelin-like spears, wearing shining protective metal helmets and metallic waistcoats. Then came the soldiers on horseback. A little boy who was standing not too far from Omar shouted to another child in great excitement, 'We heard our parents talking last night about the Roman King who lives overseas that would finally be coming to rule and protect England.'

Omar was extremely puzzled. 'How can we have a king of England, coming to rule England, who lives in another country?' he asked Zarah. But Zarah was equally surprised by the words from the boy who had spoken. This was because she had never heard of any Roman Emperor coming from overseas to live and rule in England. Omar kept asking Zarah about this but she just kept telling him to be quiet and stop asking all those silly questions. The truth was, Zarah was actually thinking the same thing, but felt embarrassed to ask.

A very tall man with a long pointed nose who was standing nearby heard them talking and said, 'The King rules over many countries, including England, and he actually lives in Rome; but he has never been to this country before.'

'Wow!' yelled Omar, looking even more confused than ever. He could not understand it at all. 'How could one person rule so many countries?' He tried asking Zarah whether the King spoke all the languages of the people who he ruled, but once again she asked him to stop asking silly questions.

By now the Roman soldiers were getting nearer to where the children were standing. It was then that the children noticed something strange. Many of the soldiers were actually black. Omar had never seen nor imagined anything like this in his life.

He had assumed that all the Romans were white Europeans. Once again Omar turned to his older sister for help, but once again she blanked him. 'Omar, stop asking all those questions. It's embarrassing,' she shouted at him.

Omar's mind was now working overtime. 'How can this be? How come so many of the soldiers are black people? Where did they come from? Were they really Roman soldiers as well?' The questions from Omar just kept coming - and from the look on Zarah's face he could see that she was equally surprised by what they were seeing, although she tried not to show it.

'Oh,' said the same very tall man who had heard Omar's questions. 'The Roman Army is made up of people from all over the empire of Rome. Many of these soldiers are from Europe, The Middle East, and parts of Africa. This is why so many of the Roman soldiers are African.'

'But why are the Roman soldiers here?' asked Omar.

'Something has to be done about the possible invasion from the North,' the man replied.

'Wow!' shouted Omar again. 'This is exciting. We're going to be seeing a battle between England and soldiers from overseas. What country is it, mister?' he asked, turning to the man. 'Who wants to take over England?'

'It's them Caledonians,' the man replied.

'Who are they?' he asked.

'Oh be quiet, Omar,' Zarah shouted. 'Stop asking all these questions.'

However Omar could not keep quiet, as he was too excited.

'This is fun!' he shouted. 'I wish all history lessons in school could be like this.' The old man smiled and continued.

'They come from way up north over the great wall in Scotland. They have been fighting and trying to invade England. Now that our new emperor has arrived, this might help keep them to their side of the great Hadrian's Wall. I think the emperor is coming to help repair and restart the work on the great wall that was built years ago by another Roman Emperor named Hadrian.'

'Do you mean this Roman Emperor has come to help save and protect England from Scotland?' asked Zarah, who was now showing as much interest as Omar.

'That's right,' said the man.

'This will certainly help me with my homework on the Romans in Britain,' thought Omar. In the space of ten minutes he'd learned so much from this tall stranger and from the parade of Roman soldiers; he wondered why all history lessons couldn't be as interesting and fun-based as this experience they were witnessing.

The man continued to talk. 'Some of the Roman soldiers arrived in York a few weeks ago but today a much larger group will arrive, which might include the Roman Emperor called Septimius Severus.'

'King Septimius of England,' thought Omar. 'How strange was that? We never learned about him at school,' he said to Zarah.

Soon they could see thousands of soldiers marching up the road towards them. Many of them were on horseback. Zarah did not like horses and suggested that they should both move back.

There were so many soldiers marching along the road that Omar and Zarah could not see the end of the procession. It was like a never-ending stream of soldiers. 'I wonder how many soldiers there are?' Zarah asked Omar. She had suddenly woken up and was now becoming more interested by the minute.

The man who was close by said 'We have been told there are about forty

40,000

~~thousand~~ Roman soldiers coming to England.'

'No way!' exclaimed Omar. 'Forty thousand soldiers coming to protect England! This must surely be one of the largest ever invasions of England by an army. There's something we didn't learn about in our history class.'

As the procession of soldiers came closer, the carriage carrying the Roman Emperor was now clearly in view. The children were given the second shock of their lives. Omar was sure he could not be mistaken. The great Roman Emperor was half-lying down, half-sitting up in a horse-carriage. The amazing thing was that he too was an African. His face was covered with a long spiky beard and he had a very serious-looking face. As he passed the crowds he sometimes waved and nodded to the people, giving a kind of half-smile.

Even Zarah was surprised, and it was her turn to ask the question. 'Does this mean that England has an African King? I can't believe it.'

'That's right' said the man. 'I understand that he was originally from Libya in North Africa.'

The children both stood there with mouths open wide as they struggled to understand what they were seeing. They both looked at each other and found themselves repeating the following words at the same time, 'There's something we never learnt in our history class. Could this be for real?' England having an African emperor named Septimius Severus who was born in North Africa, in Libya?

As the soldiers came closer to where Omar and Zarah were

standing, they could see that some of that some of the soldiers were looking into the crowd as though they were searching for something. 'What are those soldiers looking for?' Omar asked Zarah.

'I am not sure,' she replied. It was almost as if they had lost something. Suddenly, one of the soldiers pointed to where they were standing, and another soldier beside him appeared to nod his head in agreement. The soldier who had pointed towards them came over and spoke with a strange English accent, 'Would you like to come with us? The King wants to see you.'

Omar and Zarah could not believe it. Of all the people in the crowd, the King wanted to see them. Even though it was a cold day, Omar was sweating with excitement. 'Come on, Zarah, the King wants to see us.'

Zarah was a little worried and wondered if it could be a trick. After all, the King had never even met them before. 'Why would he want to meet us?' she kept thinking.

The two soldiers seemed very friendly and beckoned them to get in the horse-drawn carriage. Omar was so excited he did not even wait for Zarah, but ran over to the carriage and jumped in. Zarah was a little scared; not just of the soldiers but also of the horses, which always terrified her. But soon she too was in the carriage, sitting beside Omar, where there were several other children who must have also been invited to meet the king. Omar was so excited at the thought that he was going to meet a Roman Emperor. There was no way his homework would suffer. He was learning so much about the Romans. From the horse-drawn carriage they could see everything much better. This included England's strange new African Roman Emperor, who was two carriages in front of them.

Omar kept staring at the African King of England with the spiky beard, who remained half-sitting up and half-lying down. He was busy talking with a few other men, who were also in his carriage. There were about a dozen other children in the same carriage as themselves.

Zarah, who was not paying as much attention to the King as Omar, noticed their carriage had started to travel much faster and they were moving away from the rest of the procession. They were on a completely different road, where there were fewer people. Suddenly two of the soldiers closed the door of the carriage and ordered everyone to be very quiet. They did not seem very friendly. It was then that Zarah realised the thing she feared might happen was actually taking place. They were being taken away. The two soldiers who had appeared so friendly a few moments before now seemed to be smiling less often, and looked very unfriendly. Zarah tried to scream but one of the men put his hand over her mouth, and told her to keep quiet, or else.

All the children in the carriage, including Omar and Zarah, were very scared, and a few of them started crying. Once again, one of the soldiers shouted at them to keep quiet. Some of the other children tried to jump out of the carriage but were held back by the soldiers. 'we want to get out' a few of them shouted.

'Be quiet!' shouted one of the soldiers. 'The King will not hurt you if you remain quiet and obey him.'

'What does the King want with us and why would he want to see us?' Omar asked. But the soldier ignored them and sat watching the group of children carefully so that no-one could escape.

They soon got into the centre of York, where they entered a court-yard with a very large building where the King was going to live. A tall Roman soldier came over to the group of children. There were now about twenty of them in total who had also been brought there. Omar was amongst the youngest, while there were one or two a little older than Zarah - perhaps fourteen or fifteen years old. The soldier spoke to the group in English, but with a foreign accent.

'The King has come to protect England's defences against the people from Scotland. He needs lots of servants to help in his palace in York, and you have been selected to serve Emperor Septimius Severus.'

'Does this mean that all these Roman soldiers and the African king are going to rule England?' Omar asked out loud to Zarah. He did not have to wait for Zarah to reply. In fact, he didn't think she knew the answer anyhow, because she looked as shocked and frightened as everyone else.

'Yes, that's right,' said the soldier that had led them to the room. 'The Roman Emperor is originally from Libya in North Africa, but rules his empire from Rome. He has also had experience in Spain and was also governor in a part of France. You don't have to worry because as long as you re obedient, the King will look after you.'

Omar immediately felt a little better 'Wow!' This is going to be so exciting. I'm going to be working for the King of England!'

'Shut up, Omar. Can't you see we've been kidnapped?' Nothing good can come from this yelled Zarah angrily.

'But we're going to be with England's new African Emperor Septimius Severus, who will look after us as the soldier just said. That can't be too bad.'

Before Zarah could respond to him, the group of children were led to another large room where they were to meet the King. He was sitting on a large wooden chair surrounded by a group of men who were his special advisors. When he saw the children he stood and walked slowly towards them with his half-smile. He was struggling to walk, and seemed to be in great pain and discomfort. Two of his advisors tried to assist him as he walked, but he brushed them aside as he limped painfully towards the group.

'I wonder what's wrong with the King's leg,' Omar whispered to Zarah.

'He's got a very bad kind of arthritis or gout, which means he finds it difficult to move about unaided,' whispered one of the Emperor's assistants. 'Now, be quiet as the King is approaching us and might want to speak to you,' he added, in a very quiet voice.

Omar and Zarah could hardly believe they were stood in the presence of the African Emperor of England. He spoke to a few of his bodyguards in a different language, and the soldier then made an announcement to the group.

'The King and his advisors have selected all of you and would like you to be trained as some of his personal servants, right here in his palace in York. Now you need to come and stand before the King as he sits and examines you.'

'But we're too young to work for a king. What about our parents and family?' Zarah asked. The soldier interpreted their questions for the Emperor, who did not seem to speak or understand English. His face was covered by his beard and his eyes and overall facial expression remained very serious.

'What is your name, little boy?' asked the soldier.

'Omar. And I'm ten years old and I can't wait to begin working for the king,' he said. Once again he felt Zarah pulling at the sleeve of his shirt for him to be quiet. He was just full of excitement. All this information would certainly help him to write a very good history project on the Romans. In fact his would be so good, not even the brightest boy in his class, Norman Baker's, would be as good.

'Is he a good king?' Omar asked.

'Of course,' said the soldier. 'He is a very brave and fearless person who has fought in many battles and will not stand for anyone to disagree with him. He is 63 years old and has many years military experience. He is the first African Emperor of the Roman Empire. In fact he recently raised the salary of soldiers by nearly 50%, so we are very happy with the King. However, I must also let you know if you are not loyal to the King he would punish you or even have you killed. The Roman Empire is very large and covers many countries, and so we need to have armies to protect the countries. This is the main reason we have come to England, travelling from Lincoln to firm up our capital here in York.'

'So what will the King be doing here in the north of England? enquired Omar.

'He needs to repair the great wall first started by Emperor Hadrian to help prevent the Caledonians from threatening to invade England. We need to bring peace to this part of the Empire.'

'I am sure both of you will make very good servants, as you are very bright,' said the soldier. Not long after that Omar and Zarah were led to a separate room where they were told they would be kept until the King decided what he wanted to do with them.

The room was cold and dark, with two large chairs and a table. Although Omar and Zarah were excited at having seen so many Roman soldiers, and were even beginning to like the new African King of England, they knew they would have to get out of there.

Later that evening, as it started to get dark, Zarah whispered to Omar 'It's time to get out of here.' At first Omar was not keen to leave, as he had visions of serving in the emperor's palace. However, he soon realised they could not stay there forever as slaves or servants of this amazing African Emperor of England.

'OK,' said Omar. 'How are we going to escape?'

'The door is shut but not locked with a key, and the Roman soldiers only check in to see if we are fine every hour or so,' Zarah whispered to Omar. 'The next time he comes and checks on us we will pretend to be asleep and then escape when he leaves the room.'

A short time later, when the soldier left the room, they both opened the door and sneaked outside the building into the main courtyard, and hid behind some bushes until a group of soldiers passed by. As soon as the coast was clear, they made a run for the main road. They ran and walked along the road for about an hour along the dirt-covered road to a point where they first saw the procession of soldiers earlier that day.

Omar and Zarah were very tired and rested for few minutes by leaning against an old oak tree. 'What do we do now?' Omar asked.

'I wish, I wish, we could get back to our treehouse,' Zarah said. Suddenly their heads felt a bit dizzy, as everything started to spin. Within seconds, they were both sitting back in their treehouse at the back of their garden. They were in a state of shock after their adventure but were also very excited. They could not believe what had just happened to them. How would they even begin to explain to their friends or family that they had just gone back nearly two thousand years in time?

Although their adventures must have taken up about twelve hours, when Zarah looked at the old clock in the corner of the room, it was only 11:55 in the morning. They had only been gone a few minutes. This was truly unbelievable. After a few minutes when everything slowly started to sink in, Omar and Zarah quickly decided that their parents and friends must not be told about their adventure.

Omar looked at the book on the floor about the Romans in Britain, and started to read it very carefully. He had become very interested in the topic, and he smiled as he thought to himself that Monday morning history class at school would be very special; he would have a lot to tell his friends about the Romans in Britain and the Emperor Septimius Severus, the African ruler of Britain.

Facts About Septimius Severus

Septimius Severus was born in Libya, North Africa, in AD 145 and became Emperor of the Roman Empire in 193.

He came to Britain in A.D.208 with the purpose of controlling the entire island, but focused in reality on curbing the Caledonian tribes from invading England.

He was not very successful in his campaign against the Caledonians, as they used guerrillas tactics and many Roman Soldiers were killed.

His main achievement in Britain was his efforts at strengthening the Roman military strength along the Hadrian's Wall, as well as working on restoring the actual wall itself.

He suffered very badly from gout, and eventually died in York 4 Feb 211.

Chapter Two: John Blanke the Black Trumpeter

'This thing is so hard,' Zarah kept saying. 'I can't get the trumpet to play properly.' The more she blew, the more she seemed to struggle to get the trumpet to make a decent sound. Omar's efforts were even worse. His trumpet sounded as though it was being strangled. Omar and Zarah had been practising the trumpet for a few weeks, but were both making very slow progress. Their music teacher had even asked the children to see if they could meet and interview another trumpeter as a way to help improve their own skills with the instrument. This was a great idea on paper - but who could they ever expect to meet in their small town of Wonderham, where nothing spectacular ever happened?

They decided to go up to the treehouse at the back of their garden. As they entered, Omar threw the trumpet angrily to one side and accidentally knocked over a pile of books. One of the books had a picture of a group of trumpeters on horse-back performing for King Henry VIII of England. Omar picked up the book and then said to Zarah, 'Don't you wish you could play like those men appear to be in this picture?'

'Yeah, but we will never be as good as they probably were. It must have taken them ages to learn to play so well that they could even perform for the King of England.'

The children stared at the picture in the book and then looked at each other and smiled. 'Are you thinking what I'm thinking?' asked Omar.

'What - you mean going back in history to meet another famous person who also happened to know how to play the trumpet? I wonder if we could do it again?' Zarah thought out loud. They both stood there, looking at the picture on the page of the book. The more they kept looking at the picture, the more they wished they could be there.

Omar and Zarah held hands and then repeated those words - 'We wish, we wish, we could be part of that history on the page.' Then something strange started to happen. The room seemed to spin and the people who were in the picture on the page started to move. Once again, the children soon found themselves as part of the history on the page.

They had gone back in time to January 1511 and they found themselves a short distance away from Westminster Palace, London. There was a very large crowd moving towards the palace. 'I wonder why so many people are heading to the palace?' Omar and Zarah thought to themselves.

A group of children shouted to Omar and Zarah 'Come on, hurry up, or else we will miss the big celebration.' Omar turned to his older sister Zarah and asked her what she thought they were talking about.

'I'm not sure,' said Zarah. 'Whatever it is, there are a lot of people here.'

Everyone was excited and shouting 'It's a boy, it's a boy. There's going to be a big celebration in honour of the King's baby boy.'

'What's all the fuss for?' asked Omar. 'Why is everyone so excited about a baby? After all, babies are born every day.'

There were hundreds of people cheering and shouting. Old and young, boys and girls - all were cheering and clapping. Omar and Zarah edged closer towards the palace, where a group of children about their own age were singing, jumping, and shouting very loudly.

'There is going to be a big party to celebrate the birth of the new prince of England!' these children kept shouting. 'King Henry VIII and Queen Catherine of Aragon are going to celebrate the birth of their son.'

'He's wanted a son so badly,' remarked a woman in the crowd. 'And now there is going to be a big celebration at Westminster Palace.'

'Look up there,' said a man wearing an old grey hat. Everyone looked up towards the window where the man was still pointing.

'I think I saw someone. I wonder if it's someone carrying the baby? Maybe we will get a chance to see the baby prince.' By now, everyone in the section where the children were standing moved in unison towards the wall that was just below the window that the man had pointed to. As the curtain moved to reveal a woman holding what appeared to be a child, the rest of the crowd seemed to rush to where the children were standing, and soon there was complete chaos as hundreds of excited people ran forward to get a better view of the new addition to the royal family.

As the people dashed forward to get a better view of what they thought might be England's new prince, Zarah found herself separated from Omar. She was extremely frightened as there were so many people, and she could not see Omar anywhere. She started to panic and shout 'Omar, where are you?' However, there was so much shouting and cheering as result of the excitement in the crowd that there was no way Omar would have heard her calling out his name. She looked around anxiously amongst the hundreds of very excited cheering faces, all looking upwards towards the window where they had seen the baby boy. She could not, however, see the one face she needed to see.

Zarah decided to move out of the crowd so she could get a better view of the crowd, and hopefully spot Omar. She went towards the side of the building. 'What if I've lost Omar and have to go back to the treehouse without him?' she thought.

As she got to the side of the building there was a large gate which opened into a courtyard which had a number of stables. There Zarah came face to face with her worst nightmare – not one, not two, but several large, mean-faced, horses. There must have been about thirty or forty of them, and they were all glaring at her. Zarah was terrified.

Zarah's fear of horses started when she was only six years old. Before that she used to be very good at horse-riding, but one evening her family had gone to see the fireworks in Central London, where hundreds of soldiers and members from the armed forces were carrying out a military display. As the sun set and the fireworks display started, one of the horses became frightened and threw his mounted military rider to the ground, and jumped into the fence where Zarah was standing. The frightened horse knocked Zarah to the ground, and this resulted in her breaking her leg. From that day she had gone from a fairly competent horse-rider to someone who was petrified of horses and would never go near one.

Now here she was, paralysed with fear, as she found herself standing only a few feet away from dozens of horses. There were grey horses, brown horses, and black horses with dark, mean, unsmiling eyes staring at her. Her head felt dizzy and she was struggling to keep standing. Any minute now, she thought, the horses would charge into her and she would be hurt. Zarah was so frightened that she began struggling to breathe. She knew she had to get away, but it was as though she was frozen to the spot. She could feel beads of perspiration on her brow. Any minute now, she would collapse to the ground. It was then that she heard a soft voice behind her.

'What are you doing here?' She turned to see a tall black man holding a trumpet in one hand.

'I got lost in the crowd, I can't find my brother and those horses are going to hurt me!' she replied.

'Don't be scared,' said the tall black stranger. 'I will help you find your brother. Don't be afraid of the horses. This one is mine. Her name is Princess, and she is very gentle.'

'Who are you? Zarah asked.

'My name is John Blanke. I am one of the musicians for the Westminster celebration at the Palace for the King's baby boy. We play as part of the group of mounted trumpeters for the King.'

'No way' said Zarah. 'I didn't realise there were black people who played the trumpet for the King of England.'

'Well, there aren't many black people who play as part of the palace trumpeters. In fact, I am the only black person in the group of mounted horse trumpeters,' John Blanke explained, smiling. 'I have played for both Henry the VII and King Henry VIII.'

'I can't believe it,' said Zarah. 'You must be very good.'

'I'm okay,' he said modestly. 'So, what's your name?'

'My name's Zarah and I got separated from my ten-year-old brother while we were in the crowd,' she said, still trembling with fear because there were so many horses around.

'Don't be frightened,' he said. 'We'll find your brother and then you'll feel better and then you won't need to worry so much.'

'That's not what I'm worried or frightened about. It's those horses. They're so big and dangerous and there are so many of them. They might hurt me again, just as they did when I was little.'

'Horses are very gentle and kind. They won't hurt you. Come over here and meet Princess. Come and touch her - she is so gentle.' Despite all that he said, Zarah's feet remained fixed to the ground and would not move. Great beads of sweat were now falling from her brow.

Then John started to talk to her about his fears of playing the trumpet in front of other people.

'There was a time when I was afraid to play the trumpet in public because people would tease me because I am black. I would get nervous of playing in front of anyone, but then I started to play for a few of my friends. After a few months I started to play more and more - and now here I am, John Blanke, the black trumpeter of England playing for King and country. Now I'm a proud black man and a member of the King's mounted trumpeters. And guess what, Zarah?' he said, with a big smile on his face.

'What?' she asked nervously.

'Very few people tease me now, and when I play I am paid 8d a day for my performances. That is what King Henry VII paid me and is also what this king has also promised to pay me.'

John Blanke came over and held her hand, and slowly led Zarah towards his horse called Princess. Each step made her knees buckle a little more. But somehow she felt at ease with this black trumpeter who was going to play for King Henry VIII. As Zarah moved nearer to Princess, she closed her eyes so she would not have to look at the horse. Zarah was expecting Princess to charge towards her, but the horse remained perfectly still. Soon, with the help of John, Zarah reached out her hand and touched the horse, but then quickly moved her hand away. Nothing happened.

'See' said John. 'All you have to do to conquer your fear is try a few small steps.' Soon she put her hand on the horse again, but this time kept it there for a few seconds longer. Again, nothing happened, and the horse remained still. It was not very long before John invited Zarah to sit on the horse. This took more effort but she did it, and within thirty minutes she was riding the horse around the courtyard. In fact, Zarah got so comfortable riding Princess, she had completely forgotten about the fact that she was officially lost and separated from her brother.

'Oh dear,' said John, 'I have spent so much time with you that I forgot I need to practise for tomorrow's celebrations. The other members of the group will be here soon.'

'Do you mean I will get the chance to see some of the other trumpeters?' Zarah inquired, interested.

'Of course. We will be playing for the King tomorrow because the palace is holding a special celebration to mark the birth of the King's son. Our group of mounted trumpeters will be performing. Soon the others will arrive for a rehearsal, and as long as you promise to be very quiet during the group rehearsal, you will be able to hear me practise before they come,' he said smiling.

'That would be great. But can you help me find my brother? He must still be in the crowd, because our parents always tell us that if we get separated we should always remain in the same place until help arrives.'

'Don't worry,' said John, 'I know how we can find your brother. There is a room upstairs above the horses' stable with a window. From up there we might be able to see your brother.'

They both climbed upstairs into a little room and looked out of the window, where they could get a good view of the crowd below which was still gathered to celebrate the birth of the royal prince. After several minutes of looking anxiously over the crowd, Zarah spotted Omar, who himself looked very worried. At first Omar could not see Zarah, but she started waving and shouting, and soon he saw her and came round to where the stables were so they could meet.

Omar soon came running into the courtyard where John and Zarah were waiting. Omar was very surprised to see Zarah standing so close to the horses.

'Zarah, be careful, there are horses about.'

'Don't worry,' she replied, 'the horses are fine. My new friend John is part of a group of musicians who play for King Henry VIII.'

'Do you still want me to play for you and give you some lessons in trumpet-playing?' John asked.

'Yes please,' the children responded.

So he got his trumpet and started to play. Zarah had never seen or heard anyone play the trumpet so beautifully. The children could not believe that in early 16th century England, a black man regularly played the trumpet for the King of England. What they really enjoyed was the fact that they had the opportunity to have a few minutes of lessons from him.

'How and when did you start playing?' Zarah asked him.

'When I was about twelve years old I heard an old man playing the trumpet, and I fell in love with the sound. It reminded me of the flute-like instrument that my father played when I was a little boy. As soon as I was able, I started playing.'

'So who taught you how to play?'

'I never had any formal lessons, just picked it up naturally. My father used to play the flute a little and so he always had one and played in the evenings. As soon as I earned enough money I bought an old trumpet. I used to play with a few other black musicians all over the East End of London. One day we played for a wedding party, and that is where someone noticed how well I played and invited me to play in another band of musicians at the King's court.'

'Are you paid for playing?' Omar asked. Zarah gave him a nudge to tell Omar to keep quiet.

But John did not seem to mind. 'Oh yes' said John. 'I am paid 8d every time I play.'

Omar and Zarah were truly amazed to think they were going to get an opportunity to play the trumpet in his presence.

'Come and have go,' John urged them. He led the children to a small room where he let them choose one of several trumpets.

'Are all these yours?' they asked him.

'Yes. I have a few trumpets that I have acquired over the years. When I started playing all those years ago I only had one, but now a have a few.'

Omar and Zarah took turns as John showed them how to play the trumpet much better than they were doing. He got them to play single notes smoothly, and then they started working on a few scales. Omar and

Zarah could not believe that in the space of one hour John had managed to help them play some simple scales much better than they had done before. The more they practised the more John got them to play each note so that it flowed smoothly into the next note, therefore making a beautiful sound.

Later John let Omar and Zarah have a go riding the horses around the stable yard while playing the trumpets. Soon after that, John Blanke, Omar and Zarah were all playing the trumpet while riding horses around the stable yard. They had become mounted trumpeters. When they finished riding, Omar asked John to explain a little more about the celebration.

'Because the King wants everyone to share in his good fortune, he has asked that a special record be kept of the celebrations. This is going to be like a picture book or large picture roll with scenes from the two-day celebrations. All of this will be recorded on a 60-foot-tall roll so that future generations can see how we celebrated this special day. But guess what the best thing is?' he asked them.

'What?' they replied, with eagerness written all over their faces.

'I am going to be represented on the large picture roll. You will see some mounted musicians on horse-back playing the trumpet, and my image will be represented. I will be one of six trumpeters represented on this very important picture roll.'

She could see that John was very excited about playing at the King's palace, as well as being shown in the picture roll.

Later that evening, a small group of men arrived and joined John for a practice session. They practised for about two hours. Omar and Zarah were very impressed to see how well the trumpeters played. They felt really inspired to be in such company.

John Blanke asked the children to come over and join the group of trumpeters, and so the children were able to ask them questions. They could not have imagined that there day which started so dreadfully boring could end up like this. Here they were, actually speaking with a group of trumpeters.

The next day there was a great celebration at Westminster Palace, and only specially-invited guests were allowed to go into the actual palace court where the day-long celebrations would take place. There were musicians, acrobats, jugglers, horse-riding, and games with plenty of food.

Omar and Zarah knew that despite the crowd of excited people they would be guaranteed a place at Westminster Palace as special guests of John the famous black trumpeter. They would be able to share in the joy of the birth of King Henry VIII's son. The thing they enjoyed the most was the procession, and the music performed by the trumpeters on mounted horseback. They kept their eyes on John all through the performance, and a few times when he saw them in the crowd he managed to give them a wink and a nod of his head.

By the end of the day, Omar and Zarah made their way back to the same place where they had originally arrived, near to the palace. When they got there they said, 'We wish, we wish, we could get back to the treehouse.' Once again, everything seemed to spin, and before they knew it they were back in the treehouse. Even though they had spent two full days away with John Blanke the black trumpeter, when they got back to the treehouse, they realised they had only been gone a few minutes.

That evening, Omar and Zarah practised very long and hard with their trumpet. Their parents wondered why the children seemed to spend all evening playing and not even asking about dinner. In fact, from that day, two things happened. First, they practised much longer and started to make great improvements. Second, Zarah's fear of horses was finally conquered. All this was made possible because of their chance meeting with John the Black trumpeter, England's only black trumpeter to play for both King Henry VII and VIII.

Facts About John Blanke

John Blanke was employed by both King Henry VII and King Henry VIII.

The treasurer of the Chambers recorded that regular payments of 8d (8 pence) were paid to John Blanke the 'blacke' trumpeter.

Following the birth of his son in 1511 King Henry VIII ordered a special tournament to be held at the Palace of Westminster.

The 60-foot tapestry picture-roll was a very expensive record made to show later generations of this great two-day festival. A drawing of a black trumpeter, believed to be John Blanke appears twice on the picture-roll.

Chapter Three: The Jamaican Guy Fawkes

It was a very cold night on November 5th, and all the children who lived on the street, along with their parents and friends, were gathered in the back garden of Omar and Zarah's family to watch the fireworks display. During that week their school had been studying and learning about Guy Fawkes and the gunpowder plot of 1605. For Omar and Zarah, however, as they stood there in their back garden watching the fireworks shoot into the night sky, they kept thinking about another amazing plot to get rid of the government of England that had also ended in failure. This was in an old hayloft in Cato Street in London, February 23rd 1820.

In fact, the background to this story really started quite by accident during the previous week, when Omar and Zarah were in their back garden watching other peoples' fireworks shooting into the air. Even though he loved seeing the brilliantly-coloured fireworks, Omar often wondered why some people started setting off fireworks weeks before Bonfire night. Some of the bangs were deafening. Omar and Zarah were really excited because they had to write a school project about Guy Fawkes and the gunpowder plot of 1605. Because it was getting colder, Omar and Zarah and a few of their friends decided to go back inside and watch the fireworks from their bedroom upstairs.

Zarah started clearing away a large pile of mathematics papers from off her bed which she had been working on that morning with very little success. At least this way they could all have a better view of the fireworks. It was then that the accident happened to Mr Graham. Mr Graham was an old retired Jamaican who lived across the road. He was a retired fireman who had originally come from Jamaica, but now lived by himself since his wife died a few years ago. He had forgotten to bring in his cat from outside and the fireworks were scaring it. The children could see him frantically running around trying to catch the cat, but he was no match for the cat, especially one that was running around frightened.

As Mr Graham stumbled around in the garden, he fell over the garden hose and banged his head. Because of the noise from the fireworks no-one heard his shouts or cries for help. Omar and Zarah saw everything, and so Zarah quickly stuffed the maths papers in her jeans pocket and she and Omar ran downstairs and across the road to Mr Graham's house. They helped him to his feet and helped him inside his house.

'Shall we call an adult or the emergency number 999?' Zarah asked Omar.

'No,' said Mr Graham, 'I will be fine now that I am sitting down. I forgot that I Maggie my old cat really hates the big bangs from the fireworks. I wish England would celebrate the plot that involved my countryman from Jamaica. At least there was no gunpowder involved.'

'You mean a Jamaican was involved with Guy Fawkes?' Omar asked.

'No - I mean a Jamaican was involved in another similar plot to overthrow the government, just like Guy Fawkes, but they did not plan to use gunpowder. All this gunpowder business is not good for poor old Maggie.'

'No way!' said Omar. 'So what happened?'

'I can't remember everything, but I remember his name was William something-or-the-other. He and a few others tried to kill members of the government with a view to ruling this country.'

'Can you imagine a small group trying to take over the country and run it?' Omar thought to himself.

'Imagine a black man being part of a group trying to overturn the government?' Mr Graham chuckled.

The children wanted to stay and ask Mr Graham more questions but realised their parents might be missing them and would start looking for them, so they returned home and informed their parents about Mr Graham's fall.

That night Omar was so excited about the fireworks he could not sleep, so he went downstairs to go on the Internet. He started doing a Google search on Guy Fawkes, who plotted against the government of England. After a few minutes he started looking to see if he could find anything about a black person in British history who tried to overthrow the government, whose first name might be William.

After about twenty minutes, Omar gave out a shout of excitement. He could not believe what he was seeing on the screen. A black person had been involved in a plot to overthrow the government in 1820! He ran upstairs to call Zarah, and soon they were both staring at the computer monitor and looking at an image of William Davidson. Omar and Zarah looked at each with that knowing smile on their faces and repeated those words, 'We wish, we wish, we could be part of that history on the page!'

Once again, the room started to spin and the picture on the computer monitor seemed to get bigger, and before they knew it the children had become part of the history on the screen. The children found themselves in a hayloft in Cato Street in London. It was February 22nd 1820.

They were in a room which was very dark. There was nothing in the room except a large old wooden bench and a few large wooden stools. A little stream of light shone brightly into the room through a small crack that was in the ceiling above them. They could also hear voices coming through the crack above them, from where they could hear men talking.

'Let's kill those dirty thieving rats and take over' said one very angry voice. This was followed by loud clapping and cheering.

'No-one must stop us from carrying out our plans,' said another person, with a high-pitched voice.

Omar and Zarah felt a little frightened, as the tone of the men's voices was rather serious and threatening. The children were not sure what to do.

'Let's climb up so we can see and hear a little from the men who were talking,' whispered Omar.

'OK' said Zarah, 'but be careful.' So they climbed up onto an old bench in the room where they could peep through the crack in the ceiling and see and hear the group of men talking. There were about ten or twelve of them. Because Omar and Zarah were in the dark room below, looking up, the children could see the part of the room where the men were talking but the men could not see the two pairs of enquiring eyes looking up at them.

They all seemed very serious-looking. One of them was black and he was doing a great deal of the talking. They could also see some rifles and other guns in the corner of the room. This made them more frightened than ever.

The men almost seemed to be quarrelling with each other. The men could not make up their mind whether they should go ahead with their plan or not.

The children could hear a few of the men speaking in quiet tones about some plans about an event at a dinner party at 39 Grosvenor Square.

The black man spoke again. This time he was almost shouting. 'We have to go through with it. It's too late to back down now. Tomorrow we have to do it. We need to kill them all and take over.'

'Are you sure, William? Are you sure they will all be there at the dinner?' they could hear another man asking. Both children looked at each other with astonishment. Could this be the same William Davidson they had discovered on the internet earlier that evening?

William Davidson was replying to the question he had been asked. 'Edwards was very clear that the Prime Minister and other government ministers in the Cabinet will be at the house, and if we go there we should be able to kill them all and take control.'

'Even if they're not all there,' said another voice, 'most of them will be. Didn't you all see the article in the newspaper that Edwards showed us? It could not be clearer. They will all be there. We must go through and kill the lot of them and then march victoriously to Downing Street and give England the government the people deserve. We cannot afford to fail like Guy Fawkes' gunpowder plot. We must succeed.'

At this point several voices were heard saying 'Yes, yes, Arthur, you are right.' Several other men were also shouting and clapping their hands in approval.

Omar looked at Zarah and whispered 'What should we do now?'

'Be quiet', she whispered back to him, 'they might hear us and we could get in trouble.'

However, poor Omar was a little shorter than Zarah and had been struggling to get a clear view of the men in the room, and so tried to reach up a little more by tip-toeing to get a better sight through the small crack in the ceiling. As he tried to reach up a little higher, the bench tilted and toppled over with a loud crash as the children fell to the floor.

Suddenly, they heard the rush of footsteps coming from the room upstairs, and then there was silence. There was nowhere for Omar and Zarah to run or escape. They both realised they were going to be in big trouble. They clung tightly to each other, their hearts beating frantically with fear. They could hear footsteps slowly coming downstairs, and the steps came closer and closer. The door opened slowly. Five men entered the room and some of them were carrying guns.

'What are you doing here?' shouted one man very angrily.

'They're spies who must have been sent to watch us,' said another man.

'What shall we do with them, Arthur?' asked one man.

'We should tie them up and then throw them in the River Thames. I am sure no-one will ever miss these two little rats.' At this point, Omar and Zarah started to cry.

'Please sir, we did not mean you any harm', Zarah sobbed. 'We just stumbled into this room'.

The black man whose name was William said, 'Okay. I'll stay here and watch them while the rest of you go ahead, and I'll join you tomorrow as planned.'

The children were led upstairs by William and the other man, who was called Arthur. They entered the same room where all the other men had been gathered before. The room was filled with old wooden furniture and a small bed in the corner.

'Sit over there by the table,' Arthur ordered angrily. 'You will both have to be locked up in this room until after we finish tomorrow evening. William will keep watch over you until I return tomorrow. If you two cause any trouble, you'll be thrown into the river.' With that, he slammed the door and went downstairs.

The children had not expected to find themselves in such danger.

'You two go and sit over there,' William ordered them. As Omar attempted to sit on the chair, both he and the chair toppled over, and for the second time that evening he fell to the floor.

'Oops!' said William in frustration and anger. 'I have been meaning to fix some of this old furniture for some time. Every day another piece falls apart. Never mind, young man, let me help you up. We will not harm you, but because you are here you have to remain in this room until we finish the job. After that you can go, because everything will be done.'

William seemed a little friendlier than Arthur and spoke with a soft voice. Strangely, Omar and Zarah felt a little more at ease with this Jamaican, who was part of the plot to overthrow the British government. This was especially so after William told them that they would not be physically harmed as long as they promised to stay quiet.

'Do you think the plot will work?' Omar asked.

'What do you mean?' asked William. He looked puzzled because he wanted to know how Omar knew about the plot.

Zarah thought she had better try to explain. 'We heard a little about your plan when we were downstairs, but we are not spies. We are very interested about British history. It really was like an accident - we did not mean to come here or to spy on you. We did not even know you would be here.' Zarah tried to explain.

'Tomorrow,' said William, 'we will have a new government, and everything will be better for all of us.'

William got some tools out of a bag in the corner and started to repair the legs on the chair that had given way when Omar sat on it. He took out a chisel, hammer, saw and some nails, and began fixing the broken leg of the chair.

Within a few minutes he had it fixed, and then started repairing the leg of another chair, and then went on to repair another table that had been leaning against the wall in the corner that was also in the room.

'Where did you learn to fix furniture?' they asked him.

'I learnt this important trade years ago. In fact I used to operate a cabinet making business in Birmingham before I came to live here in London. I just hate seeing broken furniture.'

The room was small, dark and chilly, and so Zarah put her hands in the pocket of the blue jeans she was wearing. A sheet of paper fell to the floor. As she bent to pick it up, William ran over to her in a flash and grabbed the paper from her.

'What's that? Is this what they gave you so you could report on us?' asked William.

'No, no. It's part of my maths work,' Zarah replied. 'I was struggling with my maths work, and my teacher gave me these to do - but I can't do them very well.'

'Let me see that for myself,' he said. William examined the paper for a few seconds, and then his face lit up and he looked very surprised. He suddenly seemed like a changed man.

What happened next gave the children another shock.

'I remember these,' he said to himself. 'Let me show you how to do them,' he said, smiling.

They could not believe what they were hearing. Their kidnapper, a black Jamaican who was about to take part in a major British plot, was not only a former furniture maker, but also good at maths! Furthermore, he was offering to teach Zarah how to do maths.

'How come you know how to do maths?' they asked.

'When I first came to this country from Jamaica I went to a university in Scotland, where I started studying mathematics. I never finished, though. That is one of my main regrets. Always make the best use of the opportunity you get. This is why we have to do this job tomorrow.'

As usual, Omar had a lot of questions to ask. 'What are you planning to do tomorrow night, and who were the other men?'

As the children talked with William, he seemed very interested in Zarah's maths work. He soon called her over to him and started to explain to her how to do the maths work. Zarah was stunned. When and how did this black man called William Davidson learn so much about mathematics?

Once again, he told them how he started studying maths at Edinburgh University in Scotland, but got fed up and decided to go to sea instead. In fact he also mentioned that he had even started studying law, but he had a longing to do something radical to help people.

He spent about twenty minutes helping Zarah how to do her maths work. She was amazed how much he knew, and at how good a teacher he was.

Omar tried to get more information out of William about the Plot. 'So how will you carry out the plot tomorrow?' he asked.

'Well, it's simple. Tomorrow evening we will go to 39 Grosvenor Square, where some of the government officials will be having a dinner. We will knock on the door, and when it is opened by the door-keeper we will knock him out - and then we will storm the building and get rid of all the men. We are not happy with the government, which is not really serving the interest of ordinary people, and so tomorrow night the revolution will take place.'

'What is a revolution?' Omar asked.

'This is where a group of people form a brand new type of government, where the majority of people can be better off. Tomorrow England will have a new government, which we will be forming.'

'No way!' said Omar. 'Does this mean you will be in charge of the country, just like the Prime Minister?'

'That's close to it. There will be a group of us, not just me. Tomorrow we will have a new government and a black member of the government. That will be the country's first.'

'Oh no it won't be,' said Omar. 'Have you never heard of King Septimius Severus?'

'Who?' said William.

'He was England's first black emperor.'

William seemed intrigued by this, but seemed more concerned about his task for that evening.

'But why are you not happy with the government?'

'They are not doing enough for the people, and we need and deserve more. That's why you saw all those men here earlier. Arthur Thistlewood is our leader, and I am one of the inner circle of thirteen key people in the movement who normally meet to discuss how we could make things better for the country if we were in charge.'

The children promised William they would not try to escape or make any trouble, but just remain in the other room. They realised they were on the brink of witnessing something very special.

The next day was very busy, and there were men going and coming. Some of them brought weapons such as guns and rifles and then left them with William for him to keep watch. Throughout the day a few of the men would meet and talk in quiet tones about their plans for the evening. The two men who seemed to be the leaders were Arthur and William. Omar and Zarah had to remain very quiet and out of the way.

In the evening, the children were told by William to go to bed. 'In the morning you will be allowed to leave as, by then, we would have taken over.'

'Maybe we can help keep watch?' suggested Omar and Zarah.

'No,' said William, 'it will be too dangerous. We will go to Grosvenor Square and then come back for you in the morning. Whatever happens, you must not open the door, but remain here until we come back to let you go.'

The children were then led downstairs into the ground floor room where they had first heard the group planning their attack. The building was nothing more than a hayloft, and so they were instructed to sleep on the hay in the corner and wrap themselves in blankets to keep warm. Omar and Zarah stayed up late in the hayloft in Cato Street and spoke in quiet tones, barely above a whisper.

It was later that night that it happened. The children were woken by loud shouts and bangs, which they later realised were gunshots. They ran to the large crack in the ceiling through which they could see the room. There the children could see the room filled with men as well as police, and there was much shouting as the police were saying 'Drop your arms, we are officers of the peace!'

Omar and Zarah remained out of sight. Through the crack they saw the police storm the building. Arthur Thistlewood used his sword and struck one of the policemen, who fell to the floor. At the same time William Davidson dashed towards another police officer and a fight occurred, but the police grabbed him and knocked his weapon to the ground. A few of the other men escaped out of the window. But William was led away.

In all the excitement the police had run past the children, and once William Davidson was led away, Omar and Zarah realised they needed to get away from the hayloft on Cato Street. There were police officers everywhere, and when the police saw them, they were instructed to leave the building. Outside in the cold night air Omar and Zarah walked away from the hayloft in Cato Street. Since nothing else was going to be gained from remaining there, they held hands and repeated those words 'We wish, we wish, we could get back to our treehouse.'

Back at their home a few days later, and after spending a good amount of time on the Internet doing research, the children learned that the man called Edwards, who had provided details about the dinner where the members of the British Cabinet were supposed to meet, was really a spy. He had helped to set them up. William Davidson and the four other key ringleaders of this plot were all sentenced to death.

If their plan had worked, their leader, Arthur Thistlewood, and his close friends - including William

Davidson, the Black Jamaican - might have tried to form a government to rule Britain. What an unbelievable idea!

As the children sat in their front room at their own home on the 5th of November and remembered Guy Fawkes and his failed gunpowder plot, they also kept thinking about William Davidson – Britain's Jamaican Guy Fawkes - and the rest of the men who had failed in the Cato Street plot.

Key Facts about William Davidson

William Davidson was born in Jamaica in 1781 and came to Britain at age 14.

He was involved in a number of different activities as a young man such as an apprentice to a lawyer, spending time in the navy, as well as spending a short time at Aberdeen University studying mathematics.

He set up a cabinet-making business in Birmingham, but when that failed he eventually moved to London and became very interested in radical political affairs and the social conditions in England.

He later met and became part of the movement led by Arthur Thistlewood. William Davidson was part of the inner circle of the group which attempted to overthrow the government.

Un-be-known to the group, George Edwards was a spy and informant who helped set up the rest of the group by tricking them into believing a dinner was going to be held where they could kill members of the Cabinet.

The plot failed and William Davidson and four others, including Arthur Thistlewood, were later executed.

Chapter Four: The Jamaican Nurse on the Crimean Battlefield

Omar and Zarah were sitting in the front room of their house with their parents, listening to entertaining stories from their Uncle Rudolf. They were very excited because their Uncle Rudolf always seemed to have very interesting stories about his military experiences in the British Army. He had served in a number of countries, and the children were always amazed at his knowledge of military history and wars. He was telling them about the Crimean War and mentioned the name of the contributions of Florence Nightingale who most people know about and another nurse from Jamaica, called Mary Seacole, who very few people know of. In fact, she had come back to England with no money after using up all of hers trying to help British soldiers. At one point, he explained, a special festival of appreciation was held to recognise her contributions and kindness towards British soldiers. The children became very interested, as they had never heard of Mary Seacole before.

Uncle Rudolf led them to a room, where he showed them an old book about her. Omar and Zarah wished they could meet this brave nurse. As Uncle Rudolf left the children in the room to go re-join their parents, Omar and Zarah realised they would be left alone for a while. They both looked at each other and wished they could be part of the history, where they could meet Mary Seacole.

Once again, the children repeated those words, 'We wish, we wish, to be part of the history on the page.' A familiar series of events started to happen. The room started to spin, and it was not long before the children found themselves back in time to the year 1855, on a large battlefield in the Crimea.

It was a bleak, cold, and hazy afternoon. There were hundreds of men shouting, screaming, and shooting each other. Every few seconds there was a loud explosion which shook the ground. Most of the explosions were thankfully occurring hundreds of metres away from where

Omar and Zarah were, but they were scared nonetheless. They had never been in the middle of a battlefield before. This was worse than any kind of bonfire night fireworks display they had ever seen. Omar and Zarah had been to a laser quest where they could dodge laser beams, but now they had to dodge loud explosions. They realised they were not safe, and decided they needed to escape to some kind of place for shelter and safe-keeping.

'Over there!' shouted Zarah. 'Let's run to the hedges where there are no soldiers fighting.'

As they ran towards the large hedge, they tripped over a small uneven rising in the ground. From somewhere inside the soft rising they heard a voice cry out, 'Help me. Please, someone help me. Don't leave me here alone.'

Omar and Zarah were scared, and as they got up off the ground and looked behind them, they realised the soft object they had tripped over was, in fact, a wounded soldier. His face was covered with blood, which was coming from a very bad cut on his forehead. The children felt really sorry for him and shouted to him, 'Sir, what can we do to help?'

'See if you can find a nurse or doctor.'

'Okay,' they said. 'But where should we find a nurse in the middle of a battlefield?' Omar asked. 'What kind of nurse would want to come into the middle of a battlefield?'

'Kind and caring ones who really want to help,' said a soft voice behind them. For the second time they children were given the fright of their lives.

'Please stand back so I can help him and all these other men who need attention.'

The children turned around and came face to face with a black woman with a medical bag.

'Hello,' she said with a smile. 'What are you two doing in the middle of a battlefield? This is no place for children.'

'I was going to ask you the same question,' said Omar.

'I'm here to help the sick and injured soldiers.'

'But aren't you scared?' Zarah asked her.

'Well, aren't you scared?' she replied, with a big smile.

She bent down and took some bandages out of her bag and washed away the blood from the soldier's wound. His cry for help was weaker now, and the nurse kept whispering to him 'Don't worry, I'm here to help you. What's your name?' she asked. The man faintly mumbled something, which was so quiet the nurse had to bend over him more closely to hear him.

'Thanks, Andrew,' she said. 'I'll look after you now.'

'Please look after my other men!' he cried out. Then he seemed to collapse, and the nurse took his head in her arms.

'Hey you,' she said, pointing to the children. 'You two will have to be my nursing assistants. Please dip this clean bandage in the bucket of water over there and bring it to me quickly. Andrew has lost a lot of blood and we need to stop it and help him to recover, and then attend to the rest of his soldiers.'

Before they knew it, the children were making a few trips to the large bucket of water and bringing back damp and cool cloths for the nurse.

'So, what's your name?' they asked.

'Mary' she replied. 'Mary Seacole, and I'm here to help wounded soldiers.'

Suddenly there was a loud bang, and the whole ground shook as the children and the nurse called Mary were thrown to the ground. They were all covered in the mud.

'Quick, follow me to the safe shelter,' Mary said. The children were then led by Mary to the place of shelter. Mary, to their surprise, then said, 'I will be back later. I have to go and attend to the sick and injured soldiers. You two can sit over there in the corner until I come back.'

'But isn't it too dangerous?' asked Zarah.

'Yes,' she replied 'but I have to do my duty. This is what I saved and paid my money for - to come over here from England to help the sick and injured.'

'You had to pay to come here?' Omar asked.

'Yes,' she replied, 'but I will tell you more about it later when I come back.' With that, Mary stepped out into the cold, wet, and dangerous outdoors to go and help more soldiers. About twenty minutes later she came back, and two other soldiers were carrying the wounded soldier named Andrew on a stretcher. They laid him on a bed and Mary continued to nurse him for a while, before leaving to go outside again to help other soldiers.

The children could hear the sound of cannons and gunshots as the battle raged on outside. Some of the explosions were loud and so near the temporary camp or hospital where they were sheltering that the weak building actually shook. The children were given a small bed to sleep, but with all the explosions and the constant shaking of their shelter they did not really feel tired. There were rows of beds with sick soldiers being attended to by a small group of nurses. One of the most active and popular nurses was Mary. She would not pass a soldier's bed without saying a word of encouragement. Many of them laughed and joked with her as she talked with them.

Once or twice she would go outside and then come back a few minutes later with one or two assistants, who brought back other injured soldiers. Despite the rain, the cold and the danger, Mary continued working well into the night.

When she finally came in and sat down in a chair near to the children, she spoke with them to see how they were getting on. This was an opportunity for the children to find out a little more about her. They learned that Mary was from Jamaica and that her mum practised herbal medicine, which was where she learned her first skills in practical nursing. Mary was so desperate to help look after sick people that she paid her own fare to come to the Crimea to help wounded soldiers.

'Why did you have to pay with your own money to come and look after wounded soldiers?' Zarah asked.

'It seems the British people were not comfortable with a black woman working with their soldiers. I sometimes wondered whether they would prefer people to die rather provide them with help. How many other black people do you see around here?' she asked, with a smile on her face. 'My nursing hospital is some distance away, but from this shelter I am able to help many of the soldiers on the battlefield.'

'You mean you have your own business here?' asked Zarah.

'Yes,' said Mary. 'I have my own store and accommodation not too far from here, where I am able to supply provisions to the army and look after the sick and wounded.'

'How did you manage all that?' the children asked.

'When we came here we had to manage on our own with very little help from officials, and also by using local hired labourers. In fact, we had to rely on left-over bits of lumber and metals in order to order to build this special hospital. But eventually, we managed it. We have our own shop and hospital all under one roof, where we can attend to sick soldiers and sell provisions to army officers as well.'

'Where did you train and learn your medical skills?' Omar asked Mary.

'Well, my mother used to run a nursing home in Jamaica, and I used to watch and work with her and so learned on the job. I also have a great deal of experience treating the cholera disease from when I worked in Central America.'

As Mary talked with the children, she walked around and introduced them to some of the soldiers. They seemed very thankful for her kindness.

They went over to where Andrew was lying in his bed with a bandage around his head. He seemed much more relaxed now, and thanked the children and Mary for helping him. Mary informed him that the other men in his unit were doing well and should make complete recovery. At this news, Andrew gave a big smile as he continued to thank them.

As they walked around the beds there was a very loud explosion, which landed much closer to the temporary medical shelter on the battlefield. Mary looked very concerned and said, 'We might need to move everyone back a little more. The explosions are falling too near our field hospital, and you children might need to leave here,' she said. No sooner had she uttered these words, the whole place was shaken by another very loud explosion, which shattered some of the windows and resulted in smoke filing up most of the shelter. Everyone was screaming and shouting, and the nurses were trying to move everyone to the far end of the shelter.

Mary came over to a very frightened-looking Omar and Zarah and said to them that they would need to get on the horse and carriage which would take some of the patients farther away from the battlefield. The children needed no more prompting to get away from the chaotic and smoked-filled part of the building which had just been damaged by the explosion. Omar and Zarah ran towards the back of the building where Zarah said to Omar 'we need to get away from here now. It's too dangerous.'

Do you mean going back home? We can't do that without saying goodbye to Mary Seacole.'

'If we don't leave now we will be saying goodbye for ever as we'll be killed.' As the children held hands Omar repeated the words 'I wish, I wish we can meet Mary when this is all over.' Oh dear, what had he done?

In the excitement Omar had become confused and repeated the wrong set of words. Everything around them started to spin. Before they realised what had happened, they found themselves at the Royal Surrey Garden in Kennington for a special military festival of celebration and dinner in July 1857. The children had gone forward in time by a couple of years to what seemed like a big military festival. There were thousands of people in attendance.

To the far end was a large stage where a military band was setting up to give a performance. The children did not know what the occasion was, but made their way towards the huge stage. As they got to the front of the hall, there to their amazement, sat Mary Seacole.

Omar was so excited he ran towards her. 'Mary, what are you doing here? What's happening?'

Mary did not immediately recognise them, but then she cried out 'Oh, it's you two again. I'm so glad to see you. I was very worried when you disappeared on that battlefield.'

'What is happening here?' Omar asked her.

'All my money ran out while I was in the Crimea, so the people have kindly put on this event to help raise funds so I can continue to help people. I spent all my money helping others. Now others are helping me.'

'So what will be happening at this festival?' the children asked her.

'There will be hundreds and thousands of people paying to attend this four-day festival, where military bands will be performing.'

'It is really sad to hear what happened to you, but I am glad they could all put on this military fundraising event,' replied Omar.

'I never worry about it. The Lord will provide,' she said, in her usual soft voice. As the children talked with Mary a number of other individuals, mainly ex and serving soldiers, came and expressed their appreciation for the medical help and caring she had shown to them, especially on the battlefield in the Crimea War. Several different military bands performed at this military festival.

As the evening went on, more and more people came to speak with Mary. Amazingly, the children recognised one of the soldiers. This was Andrew, who they had helped on the battlefield when they first met with Mary Seacole. Andrew had not seen them, but the children made their way towards him and soon started speaking with him.

Omar and Zarah really enjoyed their day at the military festival, especially because of the buzz and excitement from the thousands of people who had turned up to attend this occasion. After watching several performances from a variety of military bands, the children realised it was time to head back home. This time they made sure they got the words correct so they would end up back home and not somewhere else. 'We wish, we wish we could get back home.' In a matter of seconds, the room started to spin and before they knew it the children were back home.

Later that evening, as Omar and Zarah continued to listen to Uncle Rudolf talk about his military stories, they were really pleased that they had been able to be part of a military adventure of their own.

Facts About Mary Seacole

Mary Seacole was born in Jamaica in 1805 and died in 1888. As a young person she observed and learned a great deal from her mother about herbal medicine.

Mary spent time in Panama and practised treating people suffering from cholera and malaria.

Mary was prevented from travelling to the Crimea to volunteer as a nurse, but she was able to raise the money and went there to set up her own establishment dedicated to helping soldiers.

Upon returning to England she was penniless, and a special military benefit festival was held in July 1857 in honour of Mary's contribution to the soldiers in the Crimean War.

Chapter Five: Cries of a Slave Woman - Mary Prince

Omar and Zarah were fed up with the amount of work they were being asked to do around the house. Each afternoon when they came home from school they had to do household chores; tidy their bedrooms, put away their things once they had eaten, do their homework, sort out their clothes for school the next day, and then pack their school bags. The list of jobs just seemed endless. In addition to the boring weekends in Wonderham, Zarah could not understand why children had to do so many chores.

'We're being treated like slaves,' she complained to Omar. 'The more we do, the more we still have left to do,' she added.

'Mum and dad are treating us like slaves!' Omar said in agreement, as they both packed away their cups and plates from the dining table.

'We learned in our class a few weeks ago that slavery was made illegal in England years ago. It seems as though mum and dad were not aware of this ruling, which took place in the 19th century!' complained Zarah. The children had been learning about the Anti-Slavery Society, which had been formed in the 1780s. They had also been learning about the work of one of its secretaries named Thomas Pringle.

As soon as they finished clearing the things from the table, they ran to the treehouse before their parents could think of anything else for them to do. The treehouse was very untidy because their parents never asked them to keep that place tidy. There were old toys and books scattered all over the floor.

'Ouch!' cried Zarah, as she fell over an untidy pile of books. As she got up from the floor she clung to Cuddles, her soft doll which she used to keep in her bedroom. She hung fondly to Cuddles and remembered when she first received this soft doll for her 5th birthday. It was only a few days after Zarah's twelfth birthday that she finally parted company with her soft cuddly friend and put it in one of the toy boxes in their treehouse.

As she got up from the floor and brushed the dirt off her clothes, she noticed one of the books on the floor was about the slaves in the Caribbean.

There was a picture of a group of black slave women standing waist-deep in water, with very large containers on their heads. Zarah wondered what it must have been like for those women who had to work so hard. Many of them looked very sad. She tried to imagine how difficult it must have been to be a slave working all day with no rights at all.

Both of the children started looking at the pictures in the book. The more she and Omar thought about this, the more they felt they needed to find out about the experiences of people in slavery. They held hands as they repeated the words 'We wish, we wish to be part of that history on the page.' Soon the room started to spin and the page seemed to get larger, and the people in the picture started to move.

Instead of going to that exact scene which had been shown in the book, the children found themselves in London, and the year was 1830. They were in a large house - they could hear someone being beaten and loud screams coming from inside the room where this apparent brutal punishment was being administered. The screaming voice kept shouting 'Stop it, stop it!' It was a woman's voice.

Another female voice, more likely from the person administering the beating, kept shouting over and over, 'You're a worthless, lazy, and careless person.'

The screaming woman who had been on the wrong end of the beatings came running into the room where the children were, and quickly closed the door behind her before locking it with a key. Almost as soon as she did this there came a series of loud bangs on the door, accompanied by more curses and insults aimed at the woman who was now in the same room as Omar and Zarah.

The voice from the other side of the door screamed, 'You better stay in there until you can learn to work properly. You're a lazy, worthless, slave. You wait until my husband comes back tonight. You can expect even more of the same. After that, we are going to kick you out of this house for good.' With that, footsteps were heard retreating as she walked away.

The black woman who had been on the wrong end of the beatings moved slowly towards the chair in the corner of the room. She seemed to be in great pain as she moved, and slumped into it and began weeping softly. Omar and Zarah were shocked. They did not know what to do, but suddenly the woman turned and saw them.

'I didn't hear you two come in,' she said in a soft sobbing voice with a distinct Caribbean accent, as she wiped away her tears and the blood coming from a small cut on the side of her face.

'We're sorry - we don't mean to cause any trouble,' said Zarah. 'Is there anything we can do to help you? Your face is bleeding,' she added with concern.

'Why was the other woman beating you up?' Omar asked.

'That's my mistress, Mrs Woods. Ever since she bought me to work for her as her slave while we were in the Caribbean, she has done nothing but beat me almost every day. For over ten years I have lived with them, and still all I get from them is beatings and more beatings. Today she was beating me because she said the plates were not washed properly - and even though I tried to tell her otherwise, she just started hitting me with a stick.'

'We're really sorry,' said Omar. 'We simply wanted to understand what it really means to be a slave,' he added.

'A slave? Why would anyone want to learn about that for? I've been one since the day I was born, and look what it's got me. Nothing. My work is endless.' There was bitterness and sadness as she spoke. 'Now I have to wait here until he comes in later, when I will certainly receive another beating. Work and punishment is all I know. Work work work, without a word of thanks. That's all I have ever known.'

'I know what you mean,' said Omar. 'Our mum and dad treat us like slaves as well.'

'Boy! Do you even know what that word means?' the woman asked Omar. 'Your parents only want you to learn how to be responsible. My mum wanted the same for me before she was forced to sell me.'

Omar, as usual, had a lot of questions; 'You were sold? But what's your name, and why did your mum have to sell you? How terrible that must have been.'

'Well, my name is Mary. Actually, my full name is Mary Prince, because that's all we could remember of my father's name. I was born as a slave in the Bermuda in the Caribbean. My parents were slaves. What's that you're holding?' she asked, very suddenly, pointing to Zarah's soft doll, Cuddles, to which she was still clinging.

Mary Prince had a strange look on her face. 'The first thing I ever remembered about my childhood was that I was bought as a doll for my white master's daughter, Betsy Williams, when we lived in the Caribbean. She made a real fuss over me, just as I suppose you once fussed over your teddy.'

Omar and Zarah were shocked to realise that Mary Prince could have been a live doll for a white girl called Betsy Williams.

'How were you treated by your masters?' asked Zarah.

'I was treated with the utmost cruelty. I was beaten for the slightest reason. Because I spoke up as well and wanted to do things my way, I received regular beatings. All my life I have wanted to be free, and my masters Mr and Mrs Woods bring me to this strange country. I feel trapped. All I want is to be back in Antigua and join Daniel.'

'Who is Daniel?' they both asked.

'He's my husband, who is a free black man who lives in Antigua. When we got married, instead of sharing in my joy, Mrs Woods only came to me to beat me for marrying him.'

'What! You got a beating for getting married?' asked Omar and Zarah in unison.

'That's right. When you are a slave you are not allowed to do what you please. That is why you should listen to your parents. You have no idea what it is like to be a slave. Would you like to have lived my life?'

Both children shook their heads and said 'No,' at the same time.

There were tears in her eyes as she spoke. The children were very sad, and realised they had to do something to help Mary.

'Where is Daniel now?' asked Zarah.

'As far as I know, he is still in Antigua. Instead of letting me stay in the Caribbean, the Wood's family brought me here to England to continue working as their slave.'

'But I thought you said you lived in Bermuda? So when did you meet your husband and manage to marry him in

Antigua?' Zarah asked, looking very puzzled.

'As a slave, I was sold several times to different slave masters. I ended up going from one plantation owner to another. It was like going from one butcher to another, where they poked and examined me before passing me on to the next customer. Mr and Mrs Woods lived in Antigua, so that's how I met Daniel. We were so happy together.'

'Why don't you try to run away and seek help, before you get more beatings when Mr Wood comes home later? Since they are planning to kick you out, you might as well as leave now,' Zarah tried to explain.

'But where would I go?' she asked them. 'I can hardly move very well because of my rheumatism. This was not helped because of my years of working in the salt ponds in the waters of the Caribbean. I hated every minute of that job. That did nothing to help my poor old joints.'

'We have heard of a man called Mr Pringle, who is a member of the Anti-Slavery Society. They are interested in looking after the welfare and rights of slaves.'

'Are you crazy?' Mary asked them. 'Who would be interested in protecting me in this country? And how did you hear about this man and this Anti-Slavery Society? You seem too young to know all of this.'

The children did not really want to answer Mary Prince's questions about how they came to know so much about the topic. They simply promised to help Mary Prince escape.

'We will help you find Mr Pringle, but do you have any friends who could help you get to his address?'

'Well, I know a few women who might help,' she said, thoughtfully. 'Sometimes we go there to do some work. Maybe I will ask them if they know of this man you speak of named Mr Pringle of the Anti-Slavery Society.'

'Do you know where these women live?' Zarah asked.

'Yes - it's only a few minutes from here.'

'Well, why don't we go there and see if they can help you.'

'Okay,' said Mary.

A little later that evening, when everything was quiet, and before Mr Woods arrived home to give Mary what would be an even more severe beating, all three sneaked out of the house and onto the cold London street. After a few minutes they knocked on a door. It was opened by a woman who immediately recognised

Mary, and who welcomed her and the children inside.

'We will help Mary to get to Hatton Gardens at a Moravian Mission House. There she will be safe and we will be able to get her to meet Mr Pringle and the members of the Anti-Slavery Society.'

The woman said she knew where the office of the Anti-Slavery Society was located, and decided that in the morning they would take Mary there. For the first time, the children saw Mary Prince laugh and smile.

That evening, Omar and Zarah sat with the other women and Mary Prince, and talked about different aspects of her life in the Caribbean.

'Why don't you write down all your life experiences and tell it to the secretary of the Anti-Slavery Society?' suggested Zarah.

'Why would I do that?'

'Other people could learn from what you went through, and hopefully plan to bring an end to slavery.'

The conversation then shifted to other topics, and so nothing more was said about Mary's new career in writing. Soon the children knew it would be time to get back to their home.

Later that evening, when everyone was asleep, Omar and Zarah quietly got back to the treehouse in their back Garden. The next day when they were asked to carry out their household chores, there were no complaints from the children. They realised what they had to do would only take a few minutes, and could not be compared to the work of 18th and 19th century slaves. Their meeting with Mary Prince had helped to settle that issue.

Facts About Mary Prince

Mary was born in about 1788 in Bermuda. Her parents were both slaves and her father was known as Prince.

She was sold several times to different slave-owners in different Caribbean islands.

Mary Prince was bought as a present for Betsy Williams, the child of her masters. She was, therefore, a live doll.

In 1818 she was sold to John Adams Wood. She had married Daniel James, a free black man in Antigua, and in 1828 the Woods family came to England and brought Mary with them.

Her book was published in 1831, after being dictated by her to members of the Anti-Slavery Society. It was the first book by a black woman in Britain.

Chapter Six: Scotland's First Black Football Captain – Andrew Watson

The whole school had turned out for the game. The two main schools in the town were playing each other in their annual football match. Omar did not want to let his team down. After all, he was only in the side because Bruce and Roger were both injured and his team was short of players. As the forward player from the opposing team came towards the goal Omar's team was defending, Omar tackled him and got hold of the ball in the left back position. He then tried to dribble with the ball out of his penalty area, but did not see another opposing player. In a second, Omar was robbed of the ball - and to make matters worse, the forward ran towards the goal and scored.

Omar had not been concentrating and was therefore not alert enough, and now his mistake had cost his team to concede a goal. To complete his miserable performance, the coach immediately replaced him, and Omar had to spend the rest of the game watching from the sidelines. He was devastated. All he ever wanted to do was to be a good defender, but he kept making costly mistakes.

Later that evening he sat in the treehouse, wishing he could be a better footballer - especially at defending. He was alone because Zarah was in her room listening to music on her new MP3 player. He desperately wanted to get into the school team but knew this would never happen if he could not do his job properly. He sat flicking through the pages of an old football magazine which featured some of Britain's best footballers. All Omar wanted to do was to spend some quality time in the presence of at least one professional footballer. That would be one way to improve his skills.

Even though Zarah was occupied listening to music, and they had never been back in time separately, the adventurous and outgoing Omar felt he needed to do this trip alone. If only he could go back in time and have a coaching session with Britain's best footballer, who was also a defender.

'I wonder who I might meet?' he thought to himself. 'Would it be John Terry, Ashley Cole, or Rio Ferdinand?' The more he looked at the football magazine, the more he longed to meet a famous British footballer. He decided to take a chance and see who he might meet. He repeated those words, 'I wish, I wish, to be part of the history on the page.'

Within a few seconds, Omar was in the middle of a football game in the year 1882. It was a football game at Hampden Park, Scotland. There was a team in blue and white hoops. Omar had never been to a football match with such a large crowd. There were thousands of people. 'Wow!' shouted Omar. 'I wonder which two teams are playing?' he thought.

There was a man standing beside him wearing a blue and white scarf. 'Which two teams are playing?' he asked the man.

'Boy, are you mad? Everyone knows who is playing. This is our chance to beat them again,' he said with a strong Scottish accent.

'To beat who?' Omar asked him.

'Scotland beat England last year 6-1 down in London and now we want to beat them again. With Andy on our team, we can't lose.'

The man looked at Omar oddly. 'This is one of the biggest matches of the year. It's England versus Scotland. And I tell you what, the English aren't doing too well!' he chuckled.

As one of the England forwards ran with the ball towards the Scotland goal, the Scottish crowd cheered, 'Take him, Andy, take him!' It was only then that Omar noticed that the

Scottish defender called Andy was in fact a black player. Of the twenty-two players on the field, the Scottish defender named Andy was the only black player. Omar was shocked. He had never imagined that as early as 1882 there was a black player actually playing for Scotland.

'What's the name of the black player?' Omar asked the same man who was standing beside him.

Again, the man looked at Omar with a very odd expression on his face. He couldn't believe Omar did not know about this obviously famous footballer. 'Surely you've heard of Andy. He's one of the country's best footballers. His name is Andrew Watson.'

Andrew Watson was playing in the left back position and was proving to be a very good tackler with a great deal of speed. Omar was struck with just how good Andrew Watson was. None of the England forwards could get past him. He was as solid as a rock.

Omar noticed that as soon as Andrew Watson was called on to go into a tackle or make a move, he kept looking around this way and that. It was as though his head was on a spring. He seemed aware of everyone around him. He was very impressive. As Scotland scored each of their goals, the crowds roared louder and louder. The final score was Scotland - 5 England - 1, and Andrew Watson had played a major role in helping them to win.

At the end of the game, as thousands of people streamed out of the stadium, Omar made his way towards a large park where he planned to sit and relax for a while, after the exciting game where

Scotland had beaten England. As he sat there, thinking about the game, he noticed a group of boys in the distance playing football. Omar went over to them and asked if he could join them for a game and before long he was engrossed in his game. As he played with the other boys, Omar tried to remember how Andrew Watson kept looking around so he could focus on those around him. As one of the other boys came towards Omar with the ball, a voice from the sidelines shouted 'Get goal-side and keep your back to your goal.'

Omar found himself listening to the voice from the sideline and prevented the player from scoring. The same voice said, 'Well done. Now keep doing that every time.'

Finally, Omar turned to see who it was that had given him such sound advice. He could not believe it. Standing a few metres away was Andrew Watson. Needless to say, the group of boys, including Omar, ran towards Andrew Watson and surrounded him.

Omar could not believe that he was standing in the presence of the black player he had been watching about forty minutes earlier.

'Wow!' said Omar. 'You were fantastic. I never realised there were any black players on the Scottish national football team.'

'Thank you,' Andrew replied. 'To be honest, there aren't many black players. I am the only one in the team. I am the first ever black player to play for a British national team.'

'I wish I could play like you and improve my defending skills when I play football so attackers can't get past me too easily.'

'Well, okay - let me help you for a little while.'

The other boys seemed shy to ask Andrew Watson any questions but, as usual, Omar was not shy in coming forward.

'Where are you from?' Omar asked him.

'I am originally from Guyana, but my father and grandfather were of Scottish origin and my mum was a local woman from Guyana.'

'How long have you been playing?' asked Omar.

'Since I was a little boy at the Kings' College School in London,' Andrew replied. 'I never really took the game seriously though until I was nineteen. I remember the time very well. It was soon after I had registered at Glasgow University to study natural philosophy, mathematics and engineering. My love and passion for football was too much for me, and so I started playing and never stopped.'

Andrew led the group of boys back to the field where they had been playing. When they got to the field, Andrew asked the group of boys to dribble with the ball and try to get past him. As he tackled each of the boys he talked with them about how he was tackling and some of the techniques he used. He then got the boys to switched roles and showed them how they needed to be alert and be one step ahead of their opponents by anticipating where they believed their opponents were going with the ball and narrowing down their angle.

'Above all,' Andrew kept saying, 'you must concentrate on your player and never let him get out of your sight if you have been asked to mark him.'

As the group of boys relaxed a little with Andrew Watson, they asked him more questions. 'Is this the first time you have played for Scotland?' asked one boy.

'Oh no,' said Andrew. 'I played my first game for Scotland last year, 1881. In fact, in that year I captained the team against England when we also beat them. We played in London, and it was good to be back playing football there. I also played for Scotland again a couple of days later, in Wrexham, where we beat Wales by 5-1.'

'This means you were the first black player to captain a national British team,' said Omar.

'Yes, I suppose you are right. And then today we have beaten England again 5-1. This surely makes us the best team in Britain. I actually started playing in 1874. I have been playing for the Scottish team called Queens' Park Football Club, which is the leading amateur football club in Scotland.'

'Are you involved in any other activities related to football?' asked some of the other boys.

'Yes. I am the club secretary of Queens' Park, which means I am also the first black man to work in football administration in Britain as I organise the club's affairs, schedule of games, and fundraising activities.'

'The first black player in Britain!' Omar kept thinking. 'I can't believe it,' he kept saying. 'You should have played for England.'

'Well, I lived there for a number of years and attended school there. I went to Kings' College School in London, which was a very prestigious school that had been formed as a junior department of Kings College London. I was fortunate as my father, Peter Miller, was a plantation owner in Guyana.'

The boys continued playing football with Andrew Watson for another thirty minutes. He continued to give them tips about playing and the boys, including Omar, found that they were learning quite a lot of ideas in such a short period of time.

Soon Andrew told the boys he had to go, and so the group of boys went their separate ways. Omar's head was still spinning later that evening when he returned to the treehouse in his back garden. He spent the rest of that evening practising with his football. He was determined to be successful like Andrew Watson, Scotland's first international black player and captain.

Facts About Andrew Watson

He was born in Guyana and came to the UK to study for a degree at Glasgow University in natural philosophy, mathematics and engineering.

He began playing football in 1874 and his position was full-back. In 1880 played for Glasgow against Sheffield at Bramall Lane, and his team won 1-0.

Andrew Watson played three times for Scotland between 1881-1882 and was also captain of the Scottish national team.

He was also Britain's first black football administrator when he was at Queens Park FC.

Chapter Seven: Claudia Jones and the Notting Hill Carnival

Omar and Zarah were very excited. All evening they talked of nothing else. Tomorrow they were going to the world-famous Notting Hill Carnival in London. Their family had never been before, and this was going to be a fun-filled day. Uncle Rudolf and his family were also going to be coming along and had decided to spend the night at Omar and Zarah's house. Omar and Zarah had seen pictures of this street carnival, but there were so many questions they needed answering. What kinds of costumes and parades would be on show? How many people would be there, and from which countries?

The children's Uncle Rudolf lived in London with his family, and came up to Wonderham to visit his sister, who was Omar and Zarah's mum. One thing about Uncle Rudolf was that he seemed to know everything about everything. He had served for many years as a soldier in the British Army and had been to many countries. The children loved when he came to visit them, as he always had interesting stories to tell them.

'Did I ever tell you about the time we were stationed in Trinidad and Tobago for a few weeks? Those people know how to carnival. It was so colourful and the streets were blocked with a sea of people dressed in bright costumes.'

'Uncle, do you think our Notting Hill Carnival tomorrow will be like the one you saw in Trinidad and Tobago in the Caribbean?' they asked him.

'I think the London one will be very similar to the one I saw in Trinidad and Tobago,' Uncle Rudolf answered.

'But how did Carnivals start, and what are they for?' Omar asked him.

'Well, it seems Caribbean people loved to celebrate on the streets rather than indoors, and to have parties, and probably this was how carnivals were started,' remarked Uncle Rudolf.

All of this discussion only helped to fuel the children's excitement about the trip they would be going on the very next day to the Notting Hill Carnival.

Soon Omar and Zarah went upstairs and sat in Zarah's bedroom, where they ended up talking about carnivals. 'I wonder how and why the first Caribbean carnivals were established in England?' Omar thought. 'Hey Zarah, wouldn't it be great if we could go back to the very first Caribbean street carnival in England? What do you think?'

Zarah was not really paying much attention to the chattering Omar, but started taking out a few clothes she might wear the next day. Omar flipped through some of the magazines they had been collecting about the Notting Hill Carnival. On one of the pages in one magazine, there was a short article and photo of a black woman whose name was Claudia Jones. She was described as the Caribbean Communist who was the founder of the Notting Hill Carnival.

'Hey Zarah, look at this!' Omar shouted with excitement.

'Oh Omar, be quiet. We've talked enough about carnivals - can't you see I'm trying to sort out my things to wear for tomorrow?'

'But look at this woman named Claudia. She was the person who started the Notting Hill Carnival.'

'Okay, let me see it then.' Zarah had a look at the photo of the woman, and suddenly seemed more interested in the magazine article about this black woman named Claudia Jones.

'Wouldn't it be cool to speak with her about the carnival? I'm sure she would know a little more than Uncle Rudolf,' Omar said, smiling.

The more they stared at the picture, the more they both felt they needed to meet this woman. Soon, they repeated those familiar words, 'We wish, we wish, to be part of the history on the page.'

Once again the room started to spin, and the picture on the magazine seemed to get larger. In a matter of seconds, the children found themselves in a cold dark street in the South of London, in the year 1959.

There were hundreds of people in the street. To one side was a group of mainly white young people with sticks and metal bars. To the other side was a group of mainly black young men, equally armed, and both groups were being kept apart by riot police. Both groups were hurling objects and insults at each other. The police were also taking away a few of most violent people on both sides and putting them in police vans which were parked a little distance away.

'Quick, Omar, we better try to get away. I think we made a mistake. This is definitely not a Caribbean carnival. This is a war-zone.'

'I wonder what those people are fighting about?'

'I'm not sure, but we need to keep away and stay safe.'

For once Omar did not have anything to say, but simply ran with Zarah towards the other end of the street. With stones, and glass bottles flying around, this was not the place to celebrate any kind of Caribbean Carnival.

After running a few hundred yards up the road, they found themselves standing outside a barber shop. They could still hear the shouts from the angry crowds in the distance, but at least they felt a little safer.

'Do you think those people rioting down there will end up in this part of the street?' Omar asked Zarah.

'I hope not. Anyway, we need to get off this street in order to keep safe, and also to keep warm.'

It was a January night, and bitterly cold. Because of the speed with which the children had walked and run in order to get away from the crowds of fighting youths, at first they did not notice the cold.

Now that they were standing still, they could feel the cold chill biting into their flesh.

It seemed as though there were only two sets of people around: those who were outside fighting and those people inside keeping safe and warm. But then there was Omar and Zarah, who did not belong to either group.

The children wondered where they could go in order to keep warm. This section of the street was deserted, although it was not very late in the evening.

'Why do you think we ended up here, Zarah?'

'I'm not sure, Omar. The thing is, I can't see nor hear anything that remotely resembles a Caribbean carnival. We've got to get out of this cold street before we freeze to death,' Zarah muttered miserably to herself.

'But there's nowhere to go!' Omar added. 'Where can we go to get out of this cold weather?' he cried out in desperation.

'You can come upstairs and stay in my office until your parents come to get you,' said a female voice from behind them.

Omar and Zarah turned to see who could be their female messiah. There, standing in front of them, was Claudia Jones. There was no mistaking. This was the same person they had seen in the magazine.

'Good evening, you must be Claudia Jones. We read about you in a magazine,' Zarah said.

'We're really glad to meet you,' Omar added.

Claudia looked shocked at realising the children knew her name.

'Who are you, and who sent you here to find me?'

'Well, actually, we...' but before Omar could continue, Zarah said, 'We heard about your plans to set up the Notting Hill Carnivals, and we wanted to participate because we have never been to one before.'

'Oh,' she said, with half a smile. 'You two seem to know quite a lot. The carnival is related to Notting Hill and also Nottingham, but we are having it at the St Pancras Town Hall tomorrow. You two can come inside and help us, as we have so much to do.'

'Thank you,' they replied. 'At least we will be safe from the fighting down the street.'

'Well,' said Claudia, 'That's why we have to have the carnival. We need to try to bring people together so they understand each other more. These race riots we have been having over the last few months really show how ignorant we are of each other.'

She guided the children through a small corridor, which led them above the barber shop and up to a small office. There was a desk with an old typewriter with piles of paper scattered on it. There were several other men and women in the room who were very busy packing things into boxes and other separate piles. The room also smelt of stale cigarettes. Whoever occupied this room was certainly a heavy smoker.

She beckoned them to sit down. At least this office was much warmer than the bitter cold which had greeted them outside on the street. Claudia spoke very kindly with the children.

'So tell me,' she asked them, 'how come you came to see me?'

'We are very interested to learn about Caribbean carnivals because our Uncle said the Trinidad and Tobago Carnivals are the best in the world,' said Omar.

'Trinidad and Tobago,' she said, with a great look of excitement. 'You know about Trinidad Carnivals? That's my home country. That is where I was born before we moved to the USA. Yes, your Uncle is right. Carnivals are very popular in Trinidad and the entire Caribbean.'

'So what do you do in this room?' Omar asked her.

'This is my main office, where I edit the West Indian Gazette, which is the first black newspaper in Britain. This is one of the main ways through which the black community can voice their opinions on matters that affect them.'

'Who started this paper?' asked Zarah.

'I founded the paper, and I'm also the main editor.'

For once it was Zarah who seemed to be asking the questions. She was really fascinated with Claudia Jones. 'What are all those boxes and papers in the corner?' she asked.

'Those are for the Carnival tomorrow at St Pancras Town Hall. This will be a cabaret-style event where some of the best Caribbean artists will be performing.'

'I thought you were organising a street carnival with thousands of people marching, singing, dancing and taking part with floats having excited people dressed in bright and colourful costumes?'

Claudia Jones laughed and said, 'No we will not be doing that, she laughed. Can't you see how cold it is outside? We would freeze to death. We are planning an indoor event in the town hall. Maybe one day we will have events on the streets, but this country is not ready for that yet.'

Both children looked at each other and smiled as they realised that Claudia Jones was making history without knowing it.

'How can we help for the event tomorrow?

'You two can help by sorting out the programme notes so everyone who attends tomorrow can see what is going to happen.'

For the next thirty minutes the children helped pack programmes, decoration and party items into boxes, and helped carry them downstairs to be loaded into a white van, which had now parked outside the barber shop. Soon the people left, and the children were alone with Claudia Jones.

Zarah was particularly interested in this black woman who was responsible for starting the Notting Hill Carnival, and she had so many questions which the magazine she was reading in the treehouse did not fully answer. 'Why did you have to leave America to come to Britain?'

'I was a committee member of the Communist Party of the United States, and we spoke out against the very harsh treatment being experienced by the poor, powerless men and women. Government agents felt I was a threat to national security and so I was imprisoned, and eventually forced to leave the country and come to England.'

She took out a cigarette and started smoking as she talked with the children and reflecting on her life. At least they realised who was responsible for the cigarette smell in the office.

'From when I was very young, all I ever wanted to do was to fight for the poor and the powerless.'

'Why are you not having the carnival in Notting Hill?' asked Omar.

'Notting Hill and Nottingham are important and we will be remembering and honouring the families of those who were killed in those cities because of the racial hatred and mistrust. We are holding this event tomorrow to help bring members from the Caribbean communities together, and at the same time to reach out to the white population of London and Britain in general so both communities can understand more of each other's culture. We are especially doing this event in memory of our fallen brother Kelso Cochrane, who was attacked by a group of white young men and killed.'

'And there we were thinking that carnivals were being held to help people have a party!' the children exclaimed.

Claudia Jones laughed as she explained a little more. 'But this is a time of celebration where we can showcase Caribbean talent, culture and history. This will be an indoor event in the form of a cabaret. There will be people seated to have a meal with performers and entertainers on the stage. We are expecting hundreds of people to attend, and some of the entertainers include the Boscoe Holder Dance Troupe and singer Cleo Laine.'

'So the reasons for the carnivals are really about educating and informing people about Caribbean culture and Caribbean people,' Zarah said thoughtfully.

'That's right,' said Claudia. 'The more we do this, the more people will come together, and hopefully spend less time fighting each other on the streets of Britain.'

The next day the children attended Britain's first Caribbean cabaret or carnival, at St Pancras Town Hall in London. This was very different from what they were expecting. There was a very colourful and musical event with many performers, and most people were seated at tables, rather than simply having a parade of people in bright costumes. There were hundreds of people in the hall and there was a great deal of music, food, laughter and on-stage entertainment.

This really was a fun-filled experience, although it was not what the children had expected. There were singers, different musicians and dancers as well as a mini fashion show. The children could see how it was that from this simple Caribbean event at the town hall, ideas would later be developed into the big street carnival of later years. The event went on late into the night.

However, later that evening, while everyone was having a good time inside, the children slipped outside and repeated the words, 'we wish, we wish to get back home.' In a matter of moments, they were back at home. This time, as they skimmed through the magazines about the Notting Hill Carnival, they spent more time reading about Claudia Jones. In the other room they could hear Uncle Rudolf talking excitedly. He was still talking telling tales about his time when he was in Trinidad and Tobago singing and dancing in the street to calypso music. 'I'm telling you,' he was saying to Omar and Zarah's parents, 'Caribbean people love to have these big outdoor parties, and I'm sure this is how we got the idea to have carnivals in this country.'

Omar and Zarah smiled to themselves as they realised they knew more about the real reasons behind the origin of carnivals than their uncle. More importantly, Omar and Zarah were so excited that they had met with Claudia Jones, the original person behind Britain's Notting Hill Carnivals. Their time at the Carnival tomorrow would now be very different.

Facts About Claudia Jones

Claudia Jones was born in Trinidad 1915 and died in 1964 in the UK. She was from a poor family background, and their family moved to the USA when she was about 9 years of age.

She was journalist by training and was an active committee member of the Communist Party of the United States of America (CPUSA). She spent time in prison for her communist beliefs and was deported from the USA and came to live in England in 1955.

She established the West Indian Gazette which was Britain's first Black newspaper, which argued for, amongst other things, West Indian independence and equality for all peoples.

St Pancras Town Hall 1959 was where the first Caribbean Carnival in Britain was held. This was partly due to the racial conflicts in Notting Hill and Nottingham in 1958, as well as the murder of Kelso Cochrane by a group of white youths.

Claudia Jones died in 1964 aged 49 and was buried at the Highgate Cemetery in North London next to Karl Marx, the founder of Communism.

Lightning Source UK Ltd.
Milton Keynes UK
UKOW050517220512

193013UK00001B/5/P